For Mimi and the entire Watson family.
Keep the reunions going.   W.H.

For my daughter, Lynda.   C.M.

Every summer Daddy, Mommy, my sister Andrea, and I go to Grandpa Lawrence's farm in North Carolina.

That's the time for our family reunion. All of my father's relatives are there —

cousins James and Hakim from Philadelphia,

and Delores and Lonnie.

Aunt Belle is there, too. She wears funny hats and tells funny stories that make us laugh.

Cousin Johnny claims he once played for the Harlem Globetrotters.

Of course, we don't believe him.

Great Aunt Nell is the oldest relative at the reunion. Daddy says she is almost one hundred years old. Everybody loves and respects her. Little Alshon is the youngest. Everybody loves him, too. Great Aunt Nell likes to baby-sit little Alshon.

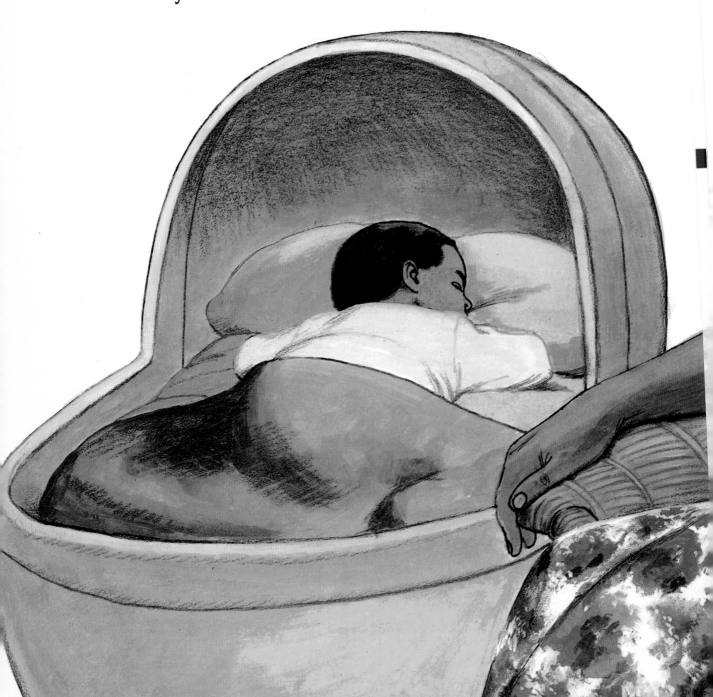

A family reunion is a special time.
It's a lot of fun, too. We go swimming.
We play ball. We pick peaches.

We sing.
And we
dance.

At night, we listen to scary stories
that Grandpa Lawrence tells.

We eat lots and lots of good food.

Every year, we put up a big poster of our family tree. It shows how all of us are related. My name is on there, too.

Our Family Tree

On the last day of the reunion, a photographer takes pictures. Grandpa Lawrence and Grandma Bert are there.

So are Uncle Tommy, my father's brother, and his family.

Aunt Linda, my father's sister, and her family are there, too.

Uncle David, my father's youngest brother, isn't married. He brings a different girlfriend to every reunion.

For our picture, I stand next to Daddy. My sister Andrea stands next to Mommy.

We have a family picture taken every year.

And every year our family gets larger.

When the family reunion is over, everyone is sad. No one wants to say good-bye. I feel sad, too. I won't get to see most of my cousins again until next summer.

But then I remember that Thanksgiving is when
my mother's family will have its reunion.
And I am happy again.

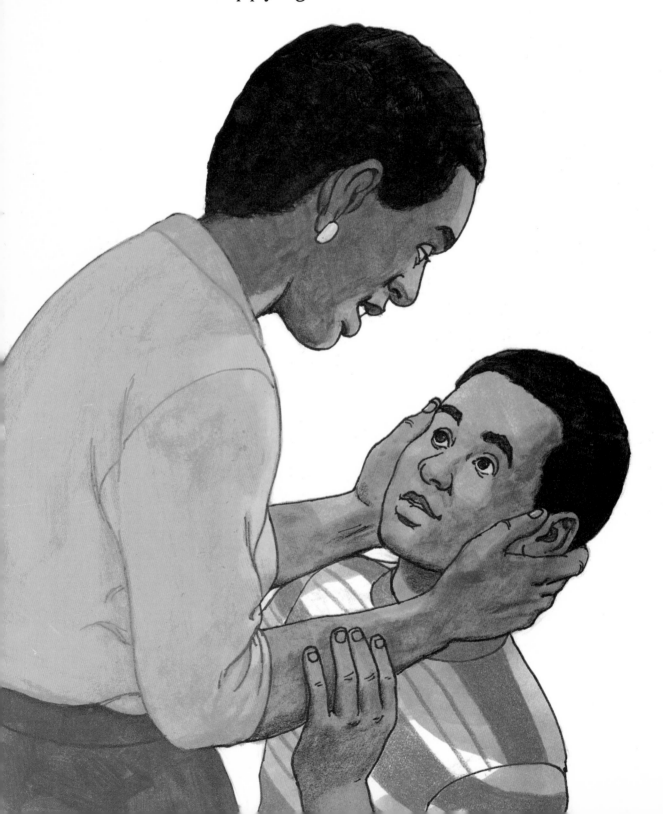

Soon it's time to say good-bye.

I love my family.

Every summer we have a family reunion!
All our relatives are there—aunts, uncles,
cousins, and Grandma and Grandpa. It's a
special time and lots of fun, too! We sing,
we dance, we eat good food, and, at night,
we listen to Grandpa tell scary stories! On
the last day we have a family picture taken.
And every year there are more people in it.

◆

I *Love My Family* introduces young
children to the importance of being a
member of a family!

RL 2 003-006

9 780590 473255

50495

ISBN 0-590-47325-5

Cartwheel
B·O·O·K·S™

SCHOLASTIC INC.

Produced by

JusT
us
BOOKS

·ABOUT THE AUTHOR·

WADE HUDSON attended Southern University in Louisiana and the Television and Film School at WNET-Channel 13 in New York City. His published works for children include the popular *Jamal's Busy Day*, *Afro-Bets Book of Black Heroes from A to Z*, *Beebe's Lonely Saturday*, and the play, *Freedom Star.* Among the plays written by Mr. Hudson that have been produced on stage are *Sam Carter Belongs Here*, *The Return*, and *A House Divided.*

A former public relations specialist, he and his wife, Cheryl, founded Just Us Books, which publishes and packages books for African-American children.

·ABOUT THE ILLUSTRATOR·

CAL MASSEY is a painter, sculptor, and illustrator. He graduated from the Hussain School of Art, where he majored in life drawing and illustration. His work is featured in numerous exhibitions and many distinguished private collections. His illustrations have appeared in textbooks, magazines, and trade books, including his first for Scholastic, *My First Kwanzaa Book.* Mr. Massey and his family live in Moorestown, New Jersey.

DATE DUE

I Love My
Family

I Love My Family

Our Family Tree

by WADE HUDSON

Illustrated by CAL MASSEY

Cartwheel
B·O·O·K·S™

SCHOLASTIC INC.

New York   Toronto   London   Auckland   Sydney

ISBN 0-590-47325-5

Text copyright © 1993 by Wade Hudson.
Illustrations copyright © 1993 by Cal Massey.
All rights reserved. Published by Scholastic Inc.
CARTWHEEL BOOKS® is a registered trademark of Scholastic Inc.

12 11 10 9 8 7 6 5   5 6 7 8/9

Printed in the U.S.A.   09